Buster Bear's Twins

Buster Bear's Twins

THORNTON W. BURGESS

With original illustrations by Harrison Cady

PUBLISHED IN ASSOCIATION WITH THE
THORNTON W. BURGESS MUSEUM AND THE
GREEN BRIAR NATURE CENTER, SANDWICH, MASSACHUSETTS
BY
DOVER PUBLICATIONS, INC., MINEOLA, NEW YORK

DOVER CHILDREN'S THRIFT CLASSICS
EDITOR OF THIS VOLUME: JILL JARNOW

Copyright

Bibliographical Note

This Dover edition, first published in 1999 in association with the Thornton W. Burgess Museum and the Green Briar Nature Center, Sandwich, Massachusetts, who have provided a new introduction, is an unabridged republication of the work originally published by Little, Brown and Company, Boston, in 1921. It contains the original Harrison Cady illustrations.

Library of Congress Cataloging-in-Publication Data

Burgess, Thornton W. (Thornton Waldo), 1874–1965.
   Buster Bear's twins / Thornton W. Burgess.
      p.   cm. — (Dover children's thrift classics)
   Summary: A pair of bear cubs share a series of adventures with the other inhabitants of the Green Forest.
   ISBN 0-486-40790-X (pbk.)
   [1. Animals—Fiction. 2. Bears—Fiction.] I. Title. II. Series.
PZ7.B917Bu   1999
[Fic]—dc21
                                            99-25510
                                               CIP

Manufactured in the United States of America
Dover Publications, Inc., 31 East 2nd Street, Mineola, N.Y. 11501

Dedication

TO CHILDHOOD

LITTLE HUMAN FOLK, LITTLE PEOPLE IN
FUR AND FEATHERS AND ALL OTHER
CHILDREN OF OLD MOTHER
NATURE THIS BOOK
IS DEDICATED

Introduction to the Dover Edition

Buster Bear's Twins introduces us to two new members of the Green Forest series. Sweet Mistress Spring's annual return to the Green Forest brings new beginnings and new life. Upon hearing that Mrs. Bear has a secret, curious Peter Rabbit wanders over one evening to her home near the great windfall to discover two baby bear cubs named Woof-Woof and Boxer. Finding it difficult to resist playing a joke on the small bear cubs, Peter frightens them so that they run, whimpering and tumbling over each other, back to the safety of their home. Suddenly, Peter's delight and glee is replaced by panic when an angry growl is heard from behind him. The reader too will soon find out that a mean spirited joke and the temptation to get even often results in mischief and mayhem for all involved.

This captivating story by Thornton W. Burgess follows the daily adventures of Woof-Woof and Boxer. Along the way they are introduced to other inhabitants of the Great World—some to their delight and dismay. You will go along with the baby cubs as they venture out with their mother, and sometimes alone, to discover many meaningful life lessons necessary to get along in the Great World. Young readers will learn about the interaction between the animals of the Green Forest in their natural habitats.

Buster Bear's Twins was first published in 1921. Thornton W. Burgess was a natural born storyteller, incorporating pearls of wisdom into his tales of nature and its creatures. Born in 1874 in Sandwich, Massachusetts, on beautiful Cape Cod, he drew on his surroundings to write stories that continue today to delight and inform readers of all ages. The founding of the Thornton W. Burgess Society

in 1976 enables his work and and writings to be appreci-
ated by several generations of readers and nature enthu-
siasts. The Society maintains a museum and a nature center, and is today a leader in environmental education on
Cape Cod and its surrounding area.

Contents

List of Illustrations

I. Mother Bear's Secret

The best kept secret soon or late
Will be found out as sure as fate.
Mother Bear.

HAVE you ever wanted to be in a number of places at the same time? Then you know exactly how Peter Rabbit felt in the beautiful springtime. You see, there was so much going on everywhere all the time that Peter felt sure he was missing something, no matter how much he saw and heard. In that he was quite right.

But you may be sure Peter did his best not to miss any more than he had to. He scampered lipperty-lipperty-lip this way, lipperty-lipperty-lip that way, and lipperty-lipperty-lip the other way, watching, listening, asking questions and making a nuisance of himself generally. For a while there were so many new arrivals in the Old Orchard and on the Green Meadows, feathered friends returning from the Sunny South and in a great hurry to begin housekeeping, and strangers passing through on their way to the Far North, that Peter hardly gave the Green Forest a thought.

But one moonlight night he happened to think of Paddy the Beaver and that he hadn't seen Paddy since before Paddy's pond froze over early in the winter.

"I must run over and pay him my respects," thought Peter.

"I certainly must. I wonder if he is as glad as the rest of us that Sweet Mistress Spring is here."

No sooner did he think of this than Peter started, lipperty-lipperty-lip, through the Green Forest for the

1

pond of Paddy the Beaver. Now the nearest way was past the great windfall where Mrs. Bear made her home. Peter hadn't thought of this when he started. He didn't think of it until he came in sight of it. The instant he saw that old windfall he stopped short. He remembered Mrs. Bear and that he had heard that she had a secret. Instantly curiosity took possession of him. He forgot all about Paddy the Beaver.

For some time Peter sat perfectly still, looking and listening. There was no sign of Mrs. Bear. Was she under that windfall in her bedroom taking a nap, or was she off somewhere? Peter wished he knew. It was such a lovely night that he had a feeling Mrs. Bear was out somewhere. A hop at a time, pausing to look and listen between hops, Peter drew nearer to the great windfall. Still there was no sign of Mrs. Bear.

With his heart going pit-a-pat, pit-a-pat, pit-a-pat, Peter drew nearer and nearer to the great windfall, and at last was close to it on the side opposite to Mrs. Bear's entrance. Taking care not to so much as rustle a dry leaf on the ground, Peter stole around the end of the great windfall until he could see the entrance Mrs. Bear always used. No one was in sight. Peter drew a long breath and hopped a little nearer. He felt very brave and bold, but you may be sure that at the same time he was ready to jump and run, as only he can at the least hint of danger.

For a long time Peter sat and stared at that entrance and wished he dared just poke his head inside. If Mrs. Bear really had a secret, it was somewhere inside there. Anyway, that is what old Granny Fox had said. He had almost worked his courage up to the point of taking just one hurried little peek in that entrance when his long ears caught a faint rustling sound under the great windfall.

Peter scurried off to a safe distance, then turned and stared at that entrance. He half expected to see Mrs. Bear's great head come poking out and he was ready to take to his heels. Instead a very small head and then another close beside it appeared.

Peter was so surprised he nearly fell over backward. Then in a flash it came to him that he knew Mrs. Bear's secret. It was out at last. Yes, sir, it was out at last. Mrs. Bear had a family! Mrs. Bear and Buster Bear had twins!

II. Peter Scares the Twins

For timid folk no joy is quite
Like giving other folks a fright.
Mother Bear.

IT isn't often that Peter Rabbit has a chance to scare any one. You know he is such a timid fellow himself that he is the one who usually gets the fright. So when he does happen to scare some one it always amuses him. Somehow he always has more respect for himself.

When on that moonlight night he discovered Mrs. Bear's secret, he had the most mixed feelings he ever had known. First came surprise, as he saw those two little heads poked out of Mrs. Bear's entrance. He was sitting up very straight and the surprise was so great that he all but tumbled over backwards. You see, there was no mistaking those two little heads for any but those of baby Bears! He knew that those were two Bear cubs, Mrs. Bear's babies, the secret she had kept hidden so long under the great windfall.

And his surprise at seeing those two little heads was only a little greater than his surprise at the smallness of them. So for perhaps two minutes Peter sat motionless, quite overcome with surprise, as he stared at those two funny little heads poked out from the entrance under the great windfall. Then all in a flash he understood the cause of Mrs. Bear's short temper and the reason she drove everybody away from there, and he felt a sudden panic of fright.

"This is no place for me," thought Peter, "and the sooner I get away from here the better." He looked hastily

4

all about. There was no sign of Mrs. Bear. Right then and there curiosity returned in full force.

"I wish those youngsters would come out where I can look at them and just see how big they are," thought Peter. "It seems safe enough here now, and perhaps if I wait a few minutes they will come out."

So Peter waited. Sure enough, in a few minutes the two little cubs did come out. Plainly it was their first glimpse of the Green Forest, and Peter almost laughed right out at the look of wonder on their faces as they stared all about in the moonlight. But not even his first surprise was greater than Peter's surprise now as he saw how small they were.

"Why," he exclaimed to himself, "why-ee, they are no bigger than I! I didn't suppose any one so big as great big Mrs. Bear could have such small children. I wonder how old they are. I wonder how big they were when they were born. I wonder if they will grow fast. I wonder if they will go about with Mrs. Bear. I suppose Buster Bear is their father, and I wonder if he ever comes to see them. They look to me rather wobbly on their legs. I wonder if Mrs. Bear told them they could come out."

And then the imp of mischief whispered to Peter. "I wonder if I can scare them," thought Peter. "It would be great fun to scare a Bear, even if it is nothing but a cub, and to scare two at once would be greater fun."

Peter suddenly thumped the ground very hard with his hind feet. It was so still there in the Green Forest that that thump sounded very loud. The two little cubs gave a startled look towards Peter. As he sat up straight in the moonlight, he looked very big. That is, he did to those two little cubs who never had seen him before.

With funny little whimpers of fright they turned and fairly tumbled over each other as they scurried back through the entrance under the great windfall. Peter laughed and laughed until his sides ached. He, Peter Rabbit, actually had frightened two Bears and made them run. Now he would have something to boast about.

III. Peter's Glee Is Short-Lived

You'll find it very seldom pays
To play a joke that works both ways.
Mother Bear.

AS two frightened little cubs ran, whimpering and tumbling over each other, for the safety of the bedroom under the great windfall, Peter Rabbit thumped twice more just by way of adding to their fright. It was most unkind of Peter. Of course. He should have been ashamed of trying to frighten babies, and those two cubs were babies and nothing more. They were baby Bears.

But Peter had so often felt little cold chills of fear chasing each other up and down his backbone in the presence of Buster Bear and Mrs. Bear that it tickled him to be able to scare any Bears, big or little. Truth to tell, it gave him a feeling as if somehow he was getting even with Buster and Mrs. Bear. Of course he wasn't. Certainly not. But he had that feeling, and he didn't once stop to think how cowardly it was to frighten babies, even though they were Bear babies.

After the two cubs had disappeared, he could hear them scrambling along under the great windfall as they hurried for the darkest corner of that dark bedroom where Mother Bear had left them when she went out to look for something to eat. All the way there they whimpered just as if they thought some dreadful enemy was after them. Peter laughed until his sides ached and the tears came to his eyes.

An angry growl right behind him put a sudden end to Peter's laughter and glee. It was his turn to run headlong

6

and to whimper as he ran. My, what jumps he made! It seemed as if his feet barely touched the ground before he was in the air again. If those little cubs had been scared, Peter was twice as scared. They had run without knowing what they ran from. But Peter knew what he was running from. He was running from an angry mother, and that mother was a Bear. It was enough to make anybody run.

Peter had been so intent on frightening those little cubs and then laughing at them that he had not heard Mother Bear until she had given that angry growl right behind him. Then he hadn't stopped to explain. Peter believes in running first and explaining later. But at the rate he was going now, there wouldn't be any explaining, because by the time he stopped Mother Bear wouldn't be near enough to hear a word he said.

The fact is Mother Bear didn't follow Peter. She simply growled once or twice in her deepest, most grumbly-rumbly voice just to add a little speed to Peter's long legs, if that were possible. Then as she watched Peter run headlong she grinned. Just as Peter had laughed at the fright of the little cubs, Mother Bear grinned at Peter's fright.

"I hope that will teach him a lesson," muttered Mrs. Bear, way down in her throat. "I don't want that long-eared bunch of curiosity hanging around here. He got a glimpse of those youngsters of mine, and now my secret will be out. Well, I suppose it would have had to be out soon."

Mrs. Bear turned into the entrance to her bedroom under the windfall, while Peter Rabbit kept on, lipperty-lipperty-lip, lipperty-lipperty-lip, through the Green Forest towards the Green Meadows and the dear Old Briar-patch. He was eager to get there and tell the news of Mrs. Bear's long-kept secret.

IV. Boxer and Woof-Woof

> 'Tis sometimes well, it seems to me,
> To see, but appear not to see.
>
> *Mother Bear.*

NOT in all the Green Forest could two livelier or more mischievous little folks be found than Boxer and Woof-Woof. Boxer was just a wee bit bigger than his sister, but he was no smarter, nor was he the least bit quicker. For more than three months they had lived under the great windfall in the Green Forest without even once poking their funny little noses outside. You see, when they were born they were very small and helpless.

And the first time they had poked their heads out, Peter Rabbit had given them a terrible scare by thumping the ground with his hind feet. Safely back in their bedroom they snuggled together.

"Who do you suppose that terrible fellow was?" whispered Woof-Woof. How that would have pleased Peter could he have heard it!

"I haven't the least idea," replied Boxer. "I guess we are lucky to be safely back here. Did you notice how his ears stood up?"

"We must ask Mother Bear about him," said Woof-Woof. "He was only about our size, and perhaps he isn't so terrible after all. Here she comes now."

"Let's not say anything about it," whispered Boxer hurriedly. "You know she told us not to go outside. We may see him again sometime and then we can ask her."

So when Mrs. Bear arrived she found Boxer and Woof-Woof curled up with their arms around each other and

8

looking as innocent as it was possible for baby Bears to look. Mother Bear grinned. She knew just what had happened out there, for she had seen it all. You remember that she had frightened Peter Rabbit even more than he had frightened the cubs. But she wisely decided that she would say nothing about it then.

"These cubs have had their first lesson in life," thought she, as she watched them trying so hard to appear to be asleep. "They disobeyed and as a result they got a great fright. I won't tell them that Peter Rabbit is one of the most harmless fellows in all the Great World. They will remember this fright longer if I don't. These scamps are growing like weeds. They went outside tonight while I was away, and that means that it is time to take them out and show them something of the Great World. If I don't, they will try it again while I am away, and something might happen to them. They are still so small that if Old Man Coyote should happen to find one of them alone I am afraid the sly old sinner would make an end of that cub."

She poked the two cubs. "You're not asleep," said she. "Don't think you can fool your mother. To-morrow morning you can go outside and play a little while, providing you will promise not to go more than one jump away from the entrance to this home of ours. There are great dangers in the Green Forest for little Bears."

Of course Boxer and Woof-Woof promised, and so for several mornings they played just outside the entrance while their mother pretended to take a nap. It was then that Chatterer the Red Squirrel and Sammy Jay and Blacky the Crow had great fun frightening those twin cubs. And they didn't know, nor did the twins, that all the time Mother Bear knew just what was going on and was keeping quiet so that the twins might learn for themselves.

V. Out in the Great World

The Great World calls, and soon or late
Must each obey and rule his fate.
Mother Bear.

NOT in all the Green Forest is there a wiser or better mother than Mrs. Bear. No one knows better than she the dangers of the Great World, or the importance of learning early in life all those things which a Bear who would live to a good old age should know. So after allowing the twins, Boxer and Woof-Woof, to play around the entrance to their home under the great windfall for a few days, she took them for their first walk in the Green Forest.

"Now," said she, as she prepared to lead the way, "you are to do just as I do. You are to follow right at my heels, and the one who turns aside for anything without my permission will be spanked. Do you understand?"

"Yes'm," replied Boxer and Woof-Woof meekly.

My, my, my, how excited they were as Mother Bear led the way out from under the old windfall! This was to be a great, a wonderful adventure. They tingled all over. They were actually going out to see something of the Great World.

The first thing Mother Bear did was to sit up and carefully test the wind with her nose. Boxer sat up and did exactly the same thing. Woof-Woof sat up and did exactly the same thing. The Merry Little Breezes tickled their noses with many scents. Mother Bear knew what each one was, but of course the twins didn't know any of them. All they knew was that they smelled good.

My, my, how excited they were as Mother Bear led the way.

Mother Bear cocked her ears forward and listened. Boxer cocked his ears forward and listened. Woof-Woof cocked her ears forward and listened. Mother Bear looked this way and looked that way. Boxer looked this way and looked that way. So did Woof-Woof.

"These are the things you must always do whenever you start out in the Great World," explained Mother Bear in her deep, grumbly-rumbly voice. "You must learn to know the meaning of every scent that reaches your nose, of every sound that reaches your ears, of everything you see, for only by such knowledge can you keep out of danger. But you must never trust your ears or your eyes only. Your nose is more to be trusted than either ears or eyes or both ears and eyes. But always use all three."

"Yes'm," replied Boxer and Woof-Woof.

Then Mother Bear started off among the great trees, shuffling along and swinging her head from side to side. Right at her heels shuffled Boxer, swinging his head from side to side, and right at his heels shuffled Woof-Woof, swinging her head from side to side. Whatever Mother Bear did the twins did. They did it because Mother Bear did it. They were keeping their promise. And little as they were, they felt very big and important, for now at last they were out in the Great World.

Chatterer the Red Squirrel saw them start out, and he chuckled as he watched those two funny little cubs do exactly as Mother Bear did. He followed along in the tree tops, jumping from tree to tree, but taking the greatest care to make no noise. He was fairly aching for a chance to scare those cubs. But as long as Mother Bear was with them, he didn't dare to try.

Mother Bear stopped and sniffed at an old log. Then she went on. Boxer stopped and solemnly sniffed at that old log. Then he went on. Woof-Woof stopped and sniffed at that old log. Then she went on. And so at last they came to a place where the earth was soft and where grew certain roots of which Mrs. Bear is very fond.

VI. The Twins Climb a Tree

Those climb the highest who have dared
To keep on climbing when most scared.
Mother Bear.

WHEN Mother Bear reached the place where grew the roots of which she was so fond, she led the twins, Boxer and Woof-Woof, over to a big tree, stood up and dug her great claws into the bark above her head. Of course Boxer did the same thing. Mother Bear gave him a push. Boxer was so surprised that without realizing what he was doing he pulled himself up a little higher, clinging to the tree with the claws of all four feet and hugging the trunk with arms and legs.

"Go right on up," said Mother Bear in her deep, grumbly-rumbly voice. "Go right on up until you reach those branches up there. There is nothing to fear. Those claws were given you for climbing, and it is time for you to learn how to use them. When you get up to those branches, you stay up there until I tell you to come down. If you don't, you will be spanked. Now up with you! Let me see you climb."

Boxer scrambled a little higher. Mother Bear turned and started Woof-Woof up after Boxer. It was a strange experience for the twins. Never before had they been above the ground, and it frightened them. They scrambled a little way then looked down and whimpered. Then they looked up at the branches above them. To Boxer and Woof-Woof those branches seemed a terrible distance up. They seemed way, way up in the sky. Really they were not very high up at all. But you remember the twins were very little, and this was their first climb.

13

So they stopped and whimpered and looked down long-ingly at the ground. But right under them stood Mother Bear, and there was a look in her eyes that told them she intended to be obeyed. Having her standing right below them gave them courage. So Boxer scrambled a little higher. Then Woof-Woof, who simply couldn't allow her brother to do anything she didn't do, scrambled a little higher. Boxer started again. Woof-Woof followed. And so at last they reached the branches. Then and not until then Mother Bear left the foot of the tree and shuffled off to dig for roots.

The instant they got hold of those branches the twins felt safe. They forgot their fears. Quite unexpectedly they felt very much at home. And of course they felt very big and bold. For a while they were content to sit and look down at the wonderful Great World. It seemed to them that from way up there they must be looking at nearly all of the Great World. Of course, they really were looking at only a very small part of the Green Forest. But it was very, very wonderful to the twins, and they looked and looked and for a long time they didn't say a word.

By and by they noticed Mother Bear digging roots some distance away. "Isn't it funny that Mother Bear has grown so much smaller?" ventured Woof-Woof.

Boxer looked puzzled. Mother Bear certainly did look smaller. Even as he watched she moved farther away, and the farther she went the smaller she seemed to be. Boxer held on with one hand and scratched his head with the other. For the first time in his life he was doing some real thinking. "I don't believe she can be any smaller," said he. "It must be she looks smaller because she is so far away. That old log down there looks smaller than it did when we stopped and sniffed at it. Some of those young trees that looked tall when we passed under them don't look tall at all now. I guess the way a thing looks depends on how near it is!"

Of course Boxer was quite right in this. He was already beginning to learn, beginning to use those lively wits which Old Mother Nature had put in that funny little head of his.

VII. A Scare That Didn't Work

Take my advice and pray beware
Of how you try to scare a Bear.
Mother Bear.

CHATTERER the Red Squirrel was indignant. He was very indignant. In fact Chatterer was angry. You know he is short-tempered and it doesn't take a great deal to make him lose his temper. He had watched Mrs. Bear and the twins start out from the great windfall and had silently followed, keeping in the tree tops as much as possible, and taking the greatest care not to let Mrs. Bear or the twins know that he was about.

Inside he had chuckled to see the twins do exactly what Mother Bear did. When she sat up and they sat up beside her, they looked so funny that he had hard work to keep from laughing right out. He had seen many funny things in the Green Forest, but nothing quite so funny as those two little Bears, hardly bigger than Peter Rabbit, gravely doing just exactly what their mother did.

So Chatterer followed, all the time hoping for a chance to give those twins a scare. But he didn't want to try it while Mother Bear was around. So he waited, hoping that she would leave them alone for a few minutes. Finally Mother Bear set the twins to climbing a tree. It was then that Chatterer became so very indignant. His sharp eyes snapped as he watched the twins scramble up that tree. He hoped they would fall. Yes, sir, Chatterer really hoped those twin cubs would fall.

You see, the trouble was that Chatterer didn't like the idea of those little Bears learning to climb trees. He felt

15

that the trees belonged to the Squirrel family. It was bad enough to have Bobby Coon and Unc' Billy Possum climbing them. Now to have two lively little Bears learning to climb was too much. It was altogether too much.

"They haven't any business in trees," sputtered Chatterer to himself, taking care not to be heard. "They haven't any business in trees. They belong on the ground, not in trees. I won't have them in the trees! I won't! I won't!"

Now of course Chatterer knew, right down in his heart, that those cubs had just as much right in the trees as had he.

The real truth of the matter was that so long as those little cubs remained on the ground, Chatterer feared them not at all. He could be as saucy and impudent to them as he pleased. He could tease them and try to scare them and feel quite safe about it, so long as their mother wasn't about. But if those cubs were going to learn to climb, and he had a feeling that they would make very good climbers, matters might be altogether different.

Chatterer watched the twins and he watched Mother Bear. At last the latter disappeared from sight. Unseen by the twins, Chatterer leaped across to the very tree in which they were sitting, but above them. "I'll give them such a scare that they will either fall down or will scramble down and never'll want to climb another tree," muttered Chatterer.

Silently he crept up behind them; then he opened his mouth and yelled at them. "Get down out of this tree!" he yelled. "Get down out of this tree!"

He was so close to those little Bears that his voice seemed to be in their very ears. They recognized it as a voice which had scared them two or three times when they had first come out of the great windfall to play. It was so close and so unexpected that it startled them so that they almost let go their hold. Then Boxer turned and for the first time had a good view of Chatterer. He was looking at a very angry Red Squirrel. But instead of being afraid and starting to scramble down from that tree, as Chatterer had expected him to do, Boxer suddenly started straight for him, and it was plain to see that Boxer was an angry small Bear.

VIII. Too Late Chatterer Is Sorry

Of yourself to hold command
Keep your temper well in hand.
Mother Bear.

THE best laid plans, even those of the smartest of Red Squirrels, sometimes go wrong. Chatterer's plan had gone wrong, just about as wrong as it could go. Those provoking twins, instead of being scared into falling or scrambling down from that tree, had been made angry and actually were starting after him. Boxer started first and Woof-Woof promptly followed. You know whatever Boxer did, Woof-Woof did.

Now Chatterer hadn't reckoned on any such thing as this happening. Not at all. And like most people who try to scare babies, Chatterer is not at all brave. Most of his bravery is in his tongue. For just an instant he was too surprised to move. Even his tongue was still. Then he turned and ran up that tree as fast as he could.

The twins came scrambling after, and they came surprisingly fast. You see, there were plenty of branches to hold on to, so they had no fear of falling. Chatterer was so scared that he didn't use those usually quick wits of his, and he ran up past the only branch of that tree that reached out near enough to another tree for him to jump across. When he thought of it, it was too late. Yes, sir, it was too late. Boxer was already standing on that very branch.

Chatterer felt then that he was trapped. He couldn't jump across to another tree. He didn't dare try to get down past those twins. He wouldn't think of jumping

18

down to the ground, unless he was actually obliged to, for it was a dreadful jump. All he could do was to climb higher and hope those twins would be afraid to follow him.

But by this time Boxer and Woof-Woof were enjoying the chase. They were enjoying the fun of climbing, and they were enjoying the discovery that they were no longer afraid of this saucy, red-coated scamp, but that he was afraid of them.

"See him run!" cried Boxer. "Come on, Woof-Woof, let's catch him! He is so small and quick that he can get about faster than we can, but we are two and he is only one. Between us we ought to be able to catch him."

Woof-Woof was quite willing, and they climbed on up after Chatterer. Chatterer's tongue was still now. He made no sound. He no longer called names. He no longer made faces. He no longer looked saucy or impudent. He looked exactly what he was, a badly scared Red Squirrel. He was sorry now that he had lost his temper and tried to scare those twins. He was very, very sorry. But it was too late. Being sorry didn't help him any now.

He was in a bad scrape, was Chatterer, and he knew it. Either of those twin Bears was much bigger than he, although they were little more than babies. They had found him out and had already discovered that they had nothing to fear from him and that he was afraid of them. It was plain to see that they were having a good time. They were enjoying the chase. Chatterer looked down at their sharp little claws and more than ever he was sorry he had not let them alone.

By this time Chatterer was clinging to the very top of that tree. If those twins came up there, he would have to make the terrible jump to the ground. He shivered as he looked down. Would those surprising twins, or one of them, be able to get up near enough to reach him?

IX. The Twins Have To Go Home

Obedience is good to see,
Especially when up a tree.
Mother Bear.

BOXER and Woof-Woof were having the best time of their short lives. Climbing was great fun. Although this was the first time they had climbed a tree, they already felt quite at home up there where the branches grew. It was fun just to climb from branch to branch. It was still greater fun to chase that red-coated little rascal who had tried to scare them out of that tree. You see, this was the first time the twins had found any one afraid of them, and it made them feel quite important. It made them feel big. They felt twice as big as when they had whimperingly started to climb that tree. So the twins were having a wonderful time.

But Chatterer the Red Squirrel was having anything but a wonderful time. He was wishing with all his might that he had kept his saucy tongue still; that he had not jumped over into that tree to try to scare those cubs; that he had not followed them in the first place; that they would become dizzy and afraid. He even wished that they would fall. The fact is, Chatterer was so badly frightened that he was capable of wishing almost anything dreadful if it would only give him a chance to escape.

Now if Chatterer had not been so badly frightened, he would have seen that Boxer, the twin who was in the lead, was already hesitating. He had reached a point where the branches were so small that they bent dangerously when he stepped on them. He had climbed as high as it was safe

20

for him to climb, and he knew it. But having set out to catch that red mischief-maker, he couldn't bear to give up. That is, he felt that if he did give up, Chatterer would boast that he had been too smart for the cubs and would make fun of them. And this is just what Chatterer would have done.

So while Chatterer was wishing with all his might that something would happen to those twins, the twins were wishing for some good excuse for stopping the chase without losing the respect they knew Chatterer now had for them.

Just then a deep, grumbly-rumbly voice came up to them from the foot of the tree. "Come down at once," said the voice. It was the voice of Mother Bear.

"Yes'm," replied Woof-Woof meekly, beginning to climb down.

"I want to catch this fellow who tried to scare us," whined Boxer, pretending that he didn't want to come down.

"You heard what I said," replied Mother Bear, and her voice was more grumbly-rumbly than before. "It is time to go home. Come down this instant."

"Yes'm," replied Boxer, and this time he said it quite as meekly as had his sister Woof-Woof. There was something in the sound of Mother Bear's voice that warned Boxer that it would be unwise to disobey.

So, with a warning to Chatterer that next time he would not get off so easily, Boxer began to climb down after Woof-Woof. When the cubs reached the lowest branches and had only the straight trunk to which to cling, they were once more afraid, and all the way down they whimpered. Somehow it was harder to climb down than up. It often is. But at last they were on the ground. Mother Bear's eyes twinkled with pride, but she took care that the cubs should not see this.

"Obedience," said she, "is the first great lesson in life. It saved you a spanking this time." Then she led the way home.

And as Boxer and Woof-Woof followed, doing exactly as she did, they heard the jeering voice of Chatterer the Red Squirrel.

"Couldn't catch me! Couldn't catch me!" jeered Chatterer.

X. The Twins Get Even with Peter Rabbit

It isn't nice; it isn't kind;
'Tis not at all the thing to do;
But those who do not take a chance
Of getting even are but few.
Mother Bear.

THIS is sad but true. It is so everywhere in the Great World, and the Great World would be a much better place in which to live if it were not so. It is the desire to get even that makes much of the trouble and the hard feeling and the unhappiness everywhere. But there are times when getting even certainly does give a lot of satisfaction. It was so with the twins Boxer and Woof-Woof.

You remember that the very first time they ventured out from under the great windfall Peter Rabbit had given them a great fright by thumping the ground with his hindfeet as only Peter can thump. The twins were so small then and they knew so little of the Great World, in fact nothing at all, that Peter had seemed to them a terrible fellow. They never had forgotten him. Whenever they were outside the great windfall, they watched for him, ready to run at sight of him.

But it was a long time before they saw Peter again, and when they did they had grown so that they were considerably bigger than he. Besides, they had been out on several trips into the Great World with Mother Bear and had learned many things, for little Bears learn very fast and have the best of memories. At last they saw Peter again. It happened this way:

Peter had stayed away from the Green Forest as long as

he could. Then curiosity to see what was going on over there had been too much for him, and he had started over to visit Paddy the Beaver. He took great care to keep away from the great windfall where Mother Bear and the twins lived. As curious as he was about those twins, and much as he wanted to see them again, he was too much afraid of Mrs. Bear and her short temper to take any chances. But he felt that it would be quite safe to visit Paddy the Beaver, for Paddy's pond was some distance from the great windfall.

Now Peter didn't know that Mother Bear was in the habit of taking the twins with her wherever she went. It just happened that this very day she had chosen to go over near the pond of Paddy the Beaver. The twins had played until they were tired and then had curled up for a nap in a sunny spot while their mother went fishing in the Laughing Brook.

When Peter arrived in sight of Paddy's pond Mother Bear was hidden behind some brush a little way up the Laughing Brook, and was sitting quietly waiting for a fish to come within reach. For once Peter was careless. He was so intent looking for Paddy the Beaver that he didn't use his eyes and ears for other things, as he should have. So he passed within a few feet of the twins without seeing them. Just beyond he sat up to look over the pond for Paddy.

Now the twins slept each with an ear open, as the saying is, and they heard Peter pass. Open flew their eyes, and they saw at once that it was the terrible fellow who had so frightened them once. But somehow he no longer looked terrible. He was smaller than they had thought. In fact, they were now considerably bigger than he. You see, they had been growing very fast. Boxer's eyes twinkled. Perhaps this fellow was like Chatterer the Red Squirrel, bold and terrible only to those who feared him. He nudged Woof-Woof. Very softly they got to their feet and stole up behind Peter.

A twig snapped under Boxer's feet. Peter turned. His

eyes seemed to pop right out of his head. With a squeal of fright, Peter jumped and started, lipperty-lipperty-lip, for the nearest pile of brush, and after him raced the twins. They knew now that this terrible fellow was more afraid of them than ever they had been of him, and they meant to get even for the fright he had given them when they were so little. It was great fun.

XI. Peter Is in a Tight Place

When you are in a place that's tight
It is no time to think of fright.
Mother Bear.

BOXER and Woof-Woof were having no end of fun. Having chased Peter Rabbit under a pile of brush, they were now trying to catch him. It was even more fun than it had been to try to catch Chatterer the Red Squirrel in the top of a tree.

But for Peter Rabbit it was no fun at all. The truth is, Peter was in a tight place and he knew it. Never had he been more badly frightened. It would have been bad enough had there been only one little Bear. Two little Bears made it more than twice as bad.

In the first place they were very lively, were those two little Bears. Peter hadn't known that little Bears could be so lively. You see, these were the first he ever had seen. The way in which they ran around that pile of brush showed how very quick on their feet they were. Peter didn't doubt that he could outrun them if he could get a fair start; the trouble was to get that fair start. He wished now that he had trusted to his long legs instead of seeking shelter under that pile of brush. He had done that in the suddenness of his fright, when the little Bears had surprised him. It is Peter's nature to seek a hiding-place in time of danger, and usually this is the wisest thing for him to do.

"I see him!" cried Boxer, poking his funny little head under the brush on one side. "I'll crawl under and drive him out to you, Woof-Woof!"

26

On the other side of the brush pile Woof-Woof danced up and down excitedly. "I'll get him! I'll get him!" she cried. "Drive him out, Boxer! Drive him out!"

"Ouch!" cried Boxer, as a sharp stick scratched his face. "He's crawling towards the end, Woof-Woof! Watch out!"

"Which end?" cried Woof-Woof, running from one end to the other and back again.

"Ouch! Wow! I'm stuck!" came the voice of Boxer. A minute later he backed out. "No use; I can't get under there," he panted. "I'll jump on top, and see if I can't scare him out that way."

So Boxer climbed up on the pile of brush and jumped up and down, while Woof-Woof ran back and forth around the edge of the pile of brush, stopping to peep under at every opening.

"I see him! I see him, Boxer!" she cried, and began to wriggle in under the brush as Boxer had done.

But she didn't go far. She soon found that Peter could get through places where she couldn't. Besides, it seemed as if sharp sticks were reaching for her from every direction. Twice she squealed as she scratched her face on them. "How do you like it," called Boxer, grinning at the sound of those squeals.

Woof-Woof backed out and brushed bits of bark from her coat, for she was much neater than her brother. "I tell you what," said she, "let's pull this pile of brush all apart. Then we'll get him."

So the twins set to work, one on one side and one on the other, to pull that pile of brush apart. Yes, Peter Rabbit certainly was in a tight place.

Boxer climbed up on the pile of brush and jumped up and down.

XII. Peter Takes a Chance

Who never takes a chance confesses
That he a coward's heart possesses.
                                        Mother Bear.

THOSE twin cubs were very much like some boys and girls. They were like them in that they were wholly thoughtless. They were having a splendid time as they tried to catch Peter Rabbit. They hadn't had so much fun for days. Not once did it pop into their funny little heads that Peter was suffering because of their fun. No, sir, they didn't once think of that.

But Peter was suffering. Peter was suffering from fright, and that kind of suffering often is worse than suffering from pain. He was sure that those cubs meant to kill him and eat him. As a matter of fact, such an idea hadn't entered the heads of the twins. You see, they were still too young to eat meat. All they were thinking of was the fun of catching Peter and getting even with him for the scare he had once given them.

Peter didn't know this. Many people had tried to catch him, and every one of them had wanted him for a dinner. So Peter was sure that this was why Boxer and Woof-Woof were trying so hard to catch him. As he dodged about under that pile of brush, his heart was in his mouth most of the time. At least, that is the way it seemed to him. But this was nothing to the way he felt when those cubs began to pull apart that pile of brush. Then for a minute despair took possession of Peter.

But it was only for a minute. Peter had been in many tight

places before, and he had learned that giving up to despair is no way to get out of tight places.

"If I stay here, they will get me," thought Peter. "If I take a chance and run they may get me, in which case I will be no worse off. But they may not get me; so I think I'll take the chance."

He listened to those excited little cubs working with might and main to pull that pile of brush apart. One was on one side and one was on the other. He might get out at either end between them and get a start before they saw him. He started to creep towards one end, but snapped a dead twig, and the quick ears of Boxer heard it. "He's coming out!" squealed Boxer, and ran around to that end.

Peter crept back to the middle. In a minute or so Boxer was back, pulling apart that brush. Then an old saying of his mother's popped into Peter's head. He had heard her say it many times when he was little and first venturing out into the Great World.

"When you must take a chance, always do the thing no one expects you to do," was what his mother had said over and over again.

"Those cubs expect me to run out at one end or the other," thought Peter. "They don't expect me to run out where either is at work. To do that will take them by surprise. It is my best chance. Yes, sir, it is my best chance."

Peter crept toward the edge where Boxer was at work tearing that brush apart. Once more his heart seemed to be in his mouth, and it was going pit-a-pat, pit-a-pat. Watching his chance, he darted out under Boxer's very nose.

XIII. A Great Mix-Up of Little Bears

If I blame you and you blame me
'Tis clear we're bound to disagree.
                                    Mother Bear.

WHEN Peter darted out under the very nose of Boxer, the little Bear was so surprised that for a couple of seconds he didn't do a thing. This was what Peter had counted on. It gave him a fair start. Then with a squeal Boxer started after him.

"He's out! He's out! Come on, Woof-Woof! We'll catch him now!" cried Boxer, and he was so excited that he stumbled over his own feet as he started after Peter.

When Peter came out from under that pile of brush, he turned to the left and started around the end of it, lipperty-lipperty-lip, as fast as he could go. Again Peter was doing the unexpected. He knew that Woof-Woof was on the other side of that pile of brush, and he knew that she knew that he knew she was there. Of course, she wouldn't expect him to run around where she was. That would be the last thing in the world she would expect.

So this is just what Peter did do. Around the end of that pile of brush, lipperty-lipperty-lip, raced Peter, with Boxer at his heels. Just as expected he met Woof-Woof running as fast as she could. Peter dodged as only Peter can. Woof-Woof was running so fast she couldn't stop instantly. Boxer was running so fast he couldn't stop.

Perhaps you can guess what happened. Those two little Bears ran into each other so hard that both were knocked over! Yes, sir, that is just what happened. Then both those little Bears lost their little tempers. They forgot all about

31

Peter Rabbit. Each blamed the other. They scrambled to their feet. Quick as a flash Boxer reached out and boxed his sister side of the head. "Why don't you look where you are going?" he snapped.

Woof-Woof was quite as quick as Boxer. Slap went one of her paws against the side of Boxer's face. "Do some looking out yourself!" she sputtered.

They stood up and danced around each other, cuffing and slapping and saying unkind things. They glared at each other with little eyes red with anger. Boxer suddenly threw his arms around Woof-Woof and upset her. Then they rolled over and over on the ground, striking, scratching, and trying to bite. First one would be on top, then the other. Over and over they tumbled, so fast that had you been there you would have seen such a mix-up of little Bears that you wouldn't have been able to tell one from the other.

It was dreadful for those twins to fight. But they had lost their tempers and there they were. You would never have guessed that they were brother and sister. After a while they were so out of breath that they had to stop.

"What are we fighting for?" asked Boxer, looking a little shame-faced as he rubbed one ear.

"I don't know," confessed Woof-Woof, rubbing her nose.

"I-I-guess I lost my temper because you ran into me," said Boxer.

"I didn't. You ran into me," declared Woof-Woof.

"No such thing!" growled Boxer, his eyes beginning to grow red again. "You ran into me."

Woof-Woof's little eyes began to snap, and I am afraid that there would have been another dreadful scene had not the memory of Peter Rabbit popped into Boxer's head just then.

"Where's that long-legged fellow we were after?" he cried. "It was all his fault."

The cubs scrambled to their feet and looked this way and that way, but Peter Rabbit was nowhere to be seen.

XIV. Two Foolish-Feeling Little Bears

Who lets his temper get away
Is bound to find it doesn't pay.
Mother Bear.

IF ever there were two foolish-feeling little Bears, the twins of Buster Bear were those two. And they looked just as foolish as they felt. While they had been fighting, Peter Rabbit had made the most of his chance and the best use of his legs and had disappeared. Where he had gone neither Boxer nor Woof-Woof had the least idea.

They looked this way. They looked that way. They peered under the pile of brush. They even tore it all apart. There was no sign of Peter. As a matter of fact, Peter was far away, headed straight for the dear Old Briar-patch; and Peter was chuckling. The instant those cubs began to fight, all fear had left Peter. He knew then that he had nothing more to fear from them.

"People who lose their tempers lose their wits with them," chuckled Peter. "I couldn't have done that better if I had planned it. My, how those cubs have grown! I think I'll keep away from that part of the Green Forest. Yes, sir, I'll keep away from there." And in that decision Peter showed that he wasn't yet too old to learn a lesson and gain wisdom therefrom.

At last the twins gave up looking for Peter. "I-I-I hope I didn't hurt you," said Boxer meekly, as he saw Woof-Woof rub her nose again. "I didn't mean to."

"Yes, you did," retorted Woof-Woof. "You did mean to hurt me. I know, because I know you felt just as I did, and I meant to hurt you. I-I-I hope I didn't."

33

"Not much," replied Boxer sheepishly as he felt of one ear.

"I guess we are even. That fellow we didn't catch probably is laughing at us and will tell everybody he meets what silly little Bears we are. I guess it doesn't pay to fight."

"That depends," said a deep, grumbly-rumbly voice. The twins turned to find Mother Bear looking at them. "It never pays to fight excepting for your rights, but the one who will not fight for his rights never will get far in the Great World. Neither will the one who is always ready to fight over nothing. Now what have you been fighting about?"

Feeling more and more foolish every minute, the twins told Mother Bear all about Peter Rabbit, how they had tried to catch him, and how they had lost their tempers when they bumped into each other.

Mother Bear's eyes twinkled, but she took care that the twins should not see that twinkle.

"You ought to be spanked, both of you," said she sternly; "and the next time I know of you fighting you will be spanked. I won't spank you this time, because I hope you have learned a lesson. When two people fight over a thing, some one else is likely to get it. People who lose their tempers usually lose more, just as you lost your chance to catch Peter Rabbit. Now all the Green Forest will laugh at you, and Peter Rabbit will boast that he was smarter than two Bears."

"We'll get even with him yet," muttered Boxer.

"No, you won't," declared Mother Bear. "Peter Rabbit will never give you a chance."

And this is exactly what Peter Rabbit had resolved himself.

XV. The Twins Meet Their Father

Beware the stranger with a smile
Lest it but hide a trickster's guile.
Mother Bear.

BOXER and Woof-Woof had begun to wonder if they and their mother were the only Bears in the Green Forest. So far they had seen no other. Then one day as they were playing about near the Laughing Brook, while Mother Bear was busy a little way off tearing open an old stump after ants, Woof-Woof discovered a footprint. She showed it to Boxer. Then the two little cubs sat up and stared at each other and their little eyes were very round with wonder.

"Mother Bear didn't make that footprint," whispered Boxer as if he were afraid of being overheard. "Who do you suppose did?"

Woof-Woof moved a little nearer to Boxer. "I haven't any idea," she whispered back, and hurriedly glanced all around. "It wasn't Mother Bear, for there is one of her footprints right over there, and it is different. There must be a great big stranger around here."

The twins drew very close together and stood up that they might better stare in every direction. They were a little frightened at the thought that a big stranger might be near. Then they remembered that Mother Bear was only a little way off, and at once they felt better. They saw no stranger. Everything about them seemed just as it should be. They cocked their little ears to listen. All they heard was the sound of Mother Bear's great claws tearing open that old stump, the cawing of Blacky the Crow far in the

35

distance, the gurgle of the Laughing Brook, and the whispering of the Merry Little Breezes in the tree tops.

Now not even Peter Rabbit has more curiosity than has a little Bear. Presently Boxer dropped down to all fours and approached that footprint. Already he had learned that his ears were better than his eyes and his nose was better than his ears. His eyes had told him nothing. His ears had told him nothing. Now he would try his nose.

He sniffed at that footprint and the hair along his shoulders rose a little. His nose told him that that footprint was made by a Bear he never had seen. There wasn't any question about it. It told him that the stranger had passed this way only a short time before. A great desire to see that stranger took possession of Boxer. Curiosity was stronger than fear.

"Let's follow his tracks; perhaps we can see him," whispered Boxer to Woof-Woof, and started along with his nose to the ground.

Now whatever one twin did, the other did. So Woof-Woof followed her brother. One behind the other, their noses to the ground, the twins stole through the Green Forest. Every once in a while Boxer sat up to look and listen. When he did this, Woof-Woof did the same thing. It was very exciting. It was so exciting that they quite forgot Mother Bear and that they had been told not to go away. So they got farther and farther from where Mother Bear was at work.

And then, without any warning at all, a great Bear stepped out from behind a fallen tree. He wore a black coat, and he was just about the size of Mother Bear. Of course you know who it was. It was Buster Bear. For the first time in their short lives the twins saw their father and he saw them. But the twins didn't know that he was their father, and he didn't know that they were his children. Things like that happen in the Green Forest.

XVI. The Twins Take to a Tree

Run while you may, nor hesitate
Lest you should prove to be too late.
Mother Bear.

MOTHER Bear is a very wise mother. One of the first things she taught the twins was that safety is the first and most important thing. Then she taught them that it is better to run away from possible danger than to wait to make sure of the danger.

"No harm comes of running away," said she, "but if you wait you may discover your danger too late to run. It is better to run away a hundred times without cause than to be too late once in time of real danger."

So when the twins suddenly came face to face with Buster Bear for the first time, they did just the right thing. For a second or two they stared at him in frightened surprise, then they turned and ran.

Do you think it queer that the twins didn't know their own father? And do you think it even more queer that Buster Bear didn't know his own children? Just remember that they had never seen him and he had never seen them before. For more than three months after they were born they hadn't been out from under that great windfall in the Green Forest. When they did come out, Buster Bear had been in another part of the Green Forest. Mother Bear had warned him to keep away from that windfall, and Buster had obeyed. So Boxer and Woof-Woof had known nothing about their father and Buster had known nothing about the twins.

Now when Buster saw those cubs, not knowing they

37

were his own, he was filled with sudden anger. He didn't want any more Bears in the Green Forest. He wanted the Green Forest just for himself and Mrs. Bear. Those young Bears were likely to make a great deal of trouble. Anyway, they would need a lot of food, and this would mean that it would be just so much harder for him to get enough to satisfy his own big appetite. So after the first surprised stare Buster growled. It was a grumbly-rumbly growl deep down in his throat. The twins heard it as they started to run, and it was the most awful sound they ever had heard.

Straight to the nearest tall tree ran the twins, and up they scrambled. Chatterer the Red Squirrel could hardly have gone up that tree faster. Somehow they felt safer in a tree than on the ground. Buster Bear walked over to the foot of the tree and looked up at the cubs. They were fat, were those cubs. They were very fat.

"They look good enough to eat," thought Buster, as he stood up at the foot of the tree, looking up at Boxer and Woof-Woof. "They would make me a very good dinner. They have no business here, anyway. I've been living on roots and such things so long that a little fresh meat would taste good. If I go up after them, I can do two things at once, rid the Green Forest of a pair of troublesome youngsters who are bound to make trouble, and get a good dinner. I believe I'll do it."

Of course this was very dreadful, but you know Buster didn't know that those cubs were his own. They meant no more to him than did Peter Rabbit, and you know he wouldn't have hesitated an instant to gobble up Peter if he had had the chance.

Buster looked all around to make sure that no one saw him. Then he dug his great claws into that tree and started to climb up.

XVII. Mother Comes to the Rescue

In all the world, below, above,
The greatest thing is mother love.
Mother Bear.

THE love of a mother is wonderful beyond all things. There is nothing to compare with it. There is nothing it will not attempt to do. There is no danger it will not face. There is no sacrifice it will not make. It is the most beautiful, the most perfect of all things.

Boxer and Woof-Woof had thought that in climbing a tall tree they were making themselves safe. It had not entered their funny little heads that great big Buster Bear would climb that tree. So you can imagine how terribly frightened they were when Buster started up that tree after them. They scrambled up and up until they were just as high as they could get. There they clung with feet and hands, the worst scared little folks in all the Green Forest.

Now little Bears are much like little boys and girls in very many ways, and one of these is their faith in mother. Another is that when they are frightened or in trouble they cry and yell for mother.

That is just what Boxer and Woof-Woof did now. The instant they saw Buster, they began to whimper and cry softly, and they kept it up as they scrambled up the trunk of that tree. But when they saw Buster Bear climbing up after them, they simply opened their mouths and bawled.

"Mamma! Mamma-a-a!" yelled Boxer, at the top of his lungs.

"Oh-o-o, mamma-a-a!" screamed Woof-Woof.

Now fortunately for the twins, Mother Bear was not so

far away that she couldn't hear them. By the sound of their voices she knew that this was no ordinary trouble they were in. Terror was in the sound of those voices. Those twins were in danger. There was no doubt about it. That danger might be danger for her as well, but she didn't give that a thought. She plunged straight in the direction from which those cries were coming, and she didn't stop to pick her way. She crashed straight through brush and branches in her way, jumped over logs, and broke down young trees.

At the sound of the first crash made by Mother Bear as she started for those cubs, Buster Bear stopped climbing. He turned his head and looked anxiously in that direction, his little ears cocked to catch every sound. At the second crash Buster Bear decided that that was no place for him. He didn't stop to climb down. He simply let go and dropped. Yes, sir, that is what he did. He let go and dropped.

It was quite a way to the ground, but the ground was where Buster Bear wanted to be, and he wanted to be there right away. He wanted to be there before whoever was coming could reach that tree. And the quickest way of getting there was to drop. A few bruises and a shaking up were nothing to Buster Bear just then.

The grunt he gave when he hit the ground even the twins heard way up in the top of the tree. It made them stop bawling for a minute to wonder if Buster had been killed. But Buster hadn't been killed. Goodness, no! In an instant he was on his feet and running away so fast that even Lightfoot the Deer would have had to do his best to keep up with him. And over his shoulder Buster Bear was throwing frightened glances.

He was not out of sight when Mother Bear burst out from among the trees. She saw him instantly. With a roar of rage, she started after Buster. Buster had seemed to be moving fast, but it was nothing compared to the way he moved when he heard that roar.

XVIII. The Twins Are Comforted

There is no comfort quite like that
Contained in mother's loving pat.
Mother Bear.

THE instant they saw Mother Bear, the twins stopped bawling. Nothing could harm them now. They knew it. Mother would take care of them. Of that there wasn't a shadow of a doubt in the minds of Boxer and Woof-Woof. Hanging on with every claw of hands and feet, they leaned out as far as they could to see what would happen to that great black Bear who had frightened them so.

But nothing happened to Buster Bear for the very good reason that he didn't wait for anything to happen. Buster was doing no waiting at all. In fact, he was moving so fast and at the same time trying to watch behind him that he didn't even pick his path. He bumped into trees and stumbled over logs in a way that to say the least was not at all dignified. But Buster was in too much of a hurry to think of dignity. There was something about the looks of Mother Bear as she tore after him that made him feel sure that he would find it much pleasanter in another part of the Green Forest, and he was in a hurry to get there.

Mother Bear didn't follow him far, only just far enough to make sure that he intended to keep right on going. Then, growling dreadful threats, she hurried back to the tree in which the cubs were. Boxer and Woof-Woof were already scrambling down as fast as they could, whimpering a little, for though they felt wholly safe now, they were not yet over their fright. She reached the foot of the tree just as they reached the ground.

41

She sat up and the twins rushed to her and snuggled as close to her as they could get. Mother Bear put a big arm around each and patted them gently. It was surprising how gentle great big Mother Bear could be.

"Wha-wha-what would that awful fellow have done to us?" asked Woof-Woof, crowding still closer to Mother Bear.

"Eaten you," growled Mother Bear, and little cold shivers ran all over Woof-Woof and Boxer.

"I hate him!" declared Boxer.

"So do I!" cried Woof-Woof. "I think he is dreadful, and I hope we'll never, never, never, see him again!"

"But you will!" replied Mother Bear. "I don't think you'll see him again right away, for he knows it isn't wise for him to hang around here when I am about. But by and by, when you are bigger, you will see him often. The fact is, he is your father."

"What!" screamed the twins, quite horrified. "That dreadful fellow our father!"

"Just so," growled Mrs. Bear. "Just so. And he isn't dreadful at all. You mustn't speak of your father that way."

"But if it isn't dreadful for a father to want to eat his own children, I guess I don't know what dreadful means," declared Boxer in a most decided tone. "I call it dreadful, and I hate him. I do so."

"Softly, Boxer. Softly," chided Mother Bear. "You see, he didn't know you were his children. He knows it now, but until he saw me coming to your rescue he didn't know it. He never had seen you before. You were simply two tempting-looking little strangers who, if I do say it, look good enough to eat." She squeezed them and patted them fondly. "His name," she added, "is Buster Bear."

XIX. The Cubs Talk It Over

Things seem good or things seem bad
According to the view you've had.
Mother Bear.

THAT is why people so often cannot agree. Each sees a
thing from a different point of view and so it looks different. Just take the case of Buster Bear and the twins.
When Boxer and Woof-Woof looked down at Buster Bear
climbing the tree after them, he seemed a terrible fellow.
But when they saw him running from Mother Bear, he
didn't seem so very terrible after all.

Of course it was a great surprise to the cubs to learn
that Buster Bear was their father. They couldn't think or
talk of anything else the rest of that day.

"Did you notice what a beautiful black coat he had?"
asked Boxer, glancing at his own little black coat with pride.

"I like brown better myself," sniffed Woof-Woof, whose
coat was brown like their mother's.

"He really is very big and handsome," continued Boxer.

"And a coward," sniffed Woof-Woof. "You noticed how
he ran from Mother Bear."

"That was because he discovered his mistake about us.
Of course he wouldn't fight then," Boxer said in defense.

"I don't care, I think he is a poor sort of a father, and I'm
not a bit proud of him," persisted Woof-Woof.

"I hope I grow up to be as big and handsome as he is.
I'm glad my coat is black," Boxer declared.

"Huh!" sniffed Woof-Woof. "A black coat may cover a
black heart. We are lucky not to be inside that black coat
of his right now."

This was true, and Boxer knew it. He wisely attempted no reply. "Where do you suppose he lives?" he ventured.

"I haven't the least idea, but I hope it isn't near here. I don't want to see him again ever," retorted Woof-Woof.

"But he is your own father," protested Boxer.

"I don't care. If all fathers are like him, I don't think much of fathers," sputtered Woof-Woof.

Mother Bear came up just in time to hear this. "Tut, tut, tut," said she. "I won't have you talking that way about your father. By and by you will know him better and learn to respect him. He is the handsomest Bear I have ever seen, and some day you will be proud that he is your father."

"I like mothers best," confided Woof-Woof, snuggling up to Mother Bear. Mother Bear's face suddenly grew very stern. "I want to know," said she, "how he happened to find you up that tree."

"We-we met him and he chased us up that tree," explained Boxer.

"And how did you happen to meet him?" persisted Mother Bear. "That tree was a long way from where I left you at play and charged you to stay."

The cubs hung their heads.

"We-we-we found his tracks and followed them," stammered Boxer in a low voice.

"And got a fright, which was no more than you deserved," declared Mother Bear. "You ought to be spanked, both of you, for your disobedience. Now you see what comes of not minding. I hope the fright you have had will be a lesson you never will forget. And don't let me hear you say another word against your father."

"No'm," replied the twins meekly.

XX. The Twins Get Their First Bath

You cannot learn to swim on land,
  So waste no time in trying.
And if you keep from getting wet
  You'll never need a drying.
                    Mother Bear.

WONDERFUL days were these for the twins, Boxer
and Woof-Woof. Every day there was something
new to see or hear or taste or smell or feel. And then
there had to be tucked away in each funny little head
where it could not be forgotten the memory of exactly
how each of these new things looked or sounded or
tasted or smelled or felt. Mother Bear was very particular about this. So, though the twins didn't know it, they
were really going to school all the time that they thought
they were simply having good times and wonderful
adventures.

One day Mother Bear led them over to the pond of
Paddy the Beaver. How the cubs did stare when they got
their first glimpse of that pond. The Laughing Brook was
the only water they were acquainted with, and in that part
of the Green Forest it was narrow and the pools were very
small. They had not supposed there was so much water in
all the Great World as now lay before them in the pond of
Paddy the Beaver.

Mother Bear led the way straight to one end of the dam
which Paddy had built to make that pond. She started
across that dam. The twins followed. Every few steps they
stopped to wonder at that pond. The Merry Little Breezes
of Old Mother West Wind were dancing across the middle

of it and making little ripples that sparkled as the Jolly Little Sunbeams kissed them.

Close to the dam the water was smooth, for the Merry Little Breezes had not come in there. Boxer and Woof-Woof looked down. Perhaps you can guess how they felt when they saw two little Bears of just their size staring back at them. The twins were so surprised that they backed away hastily. The stranger cubs did exactly the same thing. This gave Boxer and Woof-Woof confidence. They moved forward to the very edge of the dam, and there they sat up.

When they did this they lost sight of the other little Bears. They didn't know what to make of it. Then Boxer happened to look down in the water. There were the stranger cubs sitting up and doing exactly as he and Woof-Woof did. Stranger still, one of them was dressed in black and one in brown, and the latter looked so exactly like his sister that Boxer turned to look at her, to make sure that she was beside him there on the edge of the dam.

Boxer dropped down on all fours. The little stranger in black did the same thing. It provoked Boxer. Like a flash he struck at that stranger. Quick as he was, the stranger was as quick. Boxer saw a stout little paw exactly like his own coming toward him. He dodged, and as he did so his own swiftly moving little paw struck—nothing but water. It so surprised Boxer that he lost his balance, and in he tumbled with a splash.

Now Woof-Woof had been so intent on the little stranger in brown that she had paid no attention to Boxer. Woof-Woof was rather better-natured than her small brother. She had no desire to quarrel with these strangers. Slowly, very slowly, she stretched her head toward the little stranger in brown. The latter did just the same thing. They were just about to touch noses when Boxer fell in. The splash startled Woof-Woof so that she lost her balance, and in she went headfirst with a splash quite equal to that of Boxer.

If ever there were two frightened little Bears, they were

It was the first time they ever had been in the water all over.

the twins. It was the first time they ever had been in the water all over. They tried to run, but there was nothing for their feet to touch. This frightened them still more, and they made their legs go faster. Then they discovered that they were moving through the water; they were swimming! They were getting their first bath and their first swimming lesson at the same time.

XXI. The Twins Are Still Puzzled

To have true faith is to believe
E'en when appearances deceive.
Mother Bear.

IT wouldn't be quite truthful to say that the twins enjoyed that first bath and swim. They didn't. In the first place, they had gone in all over without the least intention of doing so. In fact, they had tumbled in. This had frightened them. They had opened their mouths to yell and had swallowed more water than was at all pleasant. Some of it had gone down the wrong way, and this had choked them. No, the twins didn't enjoy that first bath and swim at all.

They climbed out on the dam of Paddy the Beaver and shook themselves, making the water fly from their coats in a shower. Mother Bear had started back at the sound of the splashes they had made when they fell in, but seeing them safe, she grinned and went on about her own affairs.

"This has saved me some trouble," muttered she. "I probably would have had hard work to get them into the water without throwing them in. Now they will not be afraid of it. An accident sometimes proves a blessing."

Meanwhile the twins had shaken themselves as nearly dry as they could and were now sitting down side by side, gravely staring at the water. There was something very mysterious about that water. They felt that somehow it had played them a trick; that it was its fault that they had fallen in.

Suddenly Boxer remembered the two little stranger Bears. What had become of them? In the excitement he had forgotten all about them. He remembered that it was while striking at one of them he had fallen in. That little

49

Bear had struck at him at the same time. Boxer couldn't recall being hit or striking anything but that water. Then he had tumbled in.

But had he tumbled in? Hadn't he been pulled in? Hadn't that other little Bear grabbed him and pulled him in? The instant that idea popped into his head, Boxer was sure that that was how it all came about. He glared as much as such a little Bear could glare all around in search of that other little Bear, but no other little Bear but his sister Woof-Woof was to be seen. She was solemnly gazing at the water.

Now of course the splashing of the twins had made a lot of ripples on the surface of the water and these destroyed all reflections. But by now the water had become calm again. Woof-Woof happened to look down into it almost at her feet. A little brown Bear looked back at her. It was the same little brown Bear with whom she had tried to touch noses just before she fell into the water.

Woof-Woof poked Boxer and pointed down at the water. Boxer looked. There was that same provoking little black Bear. Boxer lifted his lips and snarled. The other little Bear lifted his lips in exactly the same way, but Boxer heard no sound save his own snarl. Boxer opened his mouth and showed all his teeth. The other little Bear opened his mouth and showed all his teeth. Whatever Boxer did, the other little Bear did. And it was just the same with Woof-Woof and the little brown Bear.

Boxer was tempted to strike at that little Bear as he had before, but just as he was about to do it, he remembered what happened before. This caused him to back away hastily. He wouldn't give that other fellow a chance to pull him in again. When he backed away, the other little Bear did the same thing. In a few steps he disappeared. Boxer cautiously stole forward. The other little Bear came to meet him.

If ever there were two puzzled little Bears they were Boxer and Woof-Woof, as they tried to get acquainted with their own reflections in the pond of Paddy the Beaver.

XXII. Boxer Gets a Spanking

Who fails to spank should have a care;
The well spanked cub, the well trained Bear.
Mother Bear.

WHEREVER Mother Bear went the twins went. In the
first place they were so full of life and mischief that
Mother Bear didn't dare leave them for any length of time.
Then, too, it was good for them to be with her, for thus
they learned many things that they could not have
learned otherwise.

But there were times when Mother Bear found Boxer
and Woof-Woof very much in the way. Such times she was
likely to send them up a tree and tell them to remain there
until her return. She always felt that they were quite safe
so long as they were up in a tree, where there was no real
mischief they could get into.

It happened that one morning Mrs. Bear sent them up a
tall pine tree with strict orders to stay there until her
return. "Don't you dare come down from that tree until I
tell you you may," said she in her deep, grumbly-rumbly
voice, as the twins scrambled up the tree.

"No'm," replied Woof-Woof meekly. But Boxer didn't say
a word.

No sooner was their mother out of sight than Boxer pro-
posed that they go down on the ground to play. "She
won't be back for some time," said he.

"By the time she does return, we will be back up here
and she will never know anything about it. Come on,
Woof-Woof."

Woof-Woof shook her head. "I'm going to stay right

51

here," said she, "and you'd better do the same thing, Boxer. If you get caught, you'll get a spanking."

"Pooh! Who cares for a spanking!" exclaimed Boxer. "Besides, I'm not going to get one. There isn't any sense in making us stay up in this tree. We can't have any fun up here. Come on down and play hide-and-seek."

But Woof-Woof wouldn't do it. "You're afraid!" declared Boxer.

"I'm not afraid!" retorted Woof-Woof indignantly. "You heard what Mother Bear said and you better mind. You may be sorry if you don't."

"Fraidy! Fraidy!" jeered Boxer, as he slid down the trunk of the tree.

Now Boxer hadn't intended to go more than a few feet from the foot of that tree. He wanted to be near enough to scramble up again at the first hint of Mother Bear's approach. But there was nothing to do down there, and without Woof-Woof to play with he found it very dull.

Little Bears are very restless and uneasy. Boxer walked round and round that tree because he could think of nothing else to do. By and by a Merry Little Breeze happened along and tickled his nose with a strange smell. The Merry Little Breezes were always doing that. Boxer used to wonder if he ever would learn all the smells of the Green Forest.

Not having anything else to do just then, Boxer decided that he would follow up that smell and find out where and what it came from. Off he started, his inquisitive little nose sniffing the air. After a little that smell grew fainter and fainter, and finally there wasn't any. You see, the Merry Little Breezes were carrying it in quite another direction.

Boxer turned to go back. He thought he was going straight toward that tree where Mother Bear had left him. But he wasn't, and by and by he discovered that he was lost. Then he began to run, and as he ran he whimpered. Suddenly out from behind a tree stepped Mother Bear.

Boxer was so glad to see her he quite forgot that he had disobeyed.

But Mother Bear didn't forget. "What are you doing here?" she demanded. Boxer hung his head and didn't say a word.

"A cub who disobeys must be punished," said Mother Bear, and she promptly gave Boxer the first real spanking he ever had received. How he did wish he had stayed up in that tree with Woof-Woof.

XXIII. Boxer Is Sulky

The world can do quite well without
The sulky folks and those who pout.
Mother Bear.

SULKY folks are not pleasant to have around. They should be put away by themselves and kept there until they are through being sulky. Now ordinarily little Bears are not sulky. It isn't their nature to be sulky. But Boxer, the disobedient little cub, was sulky. He was very sulky indeed. And it was all because of his twin sister, Woof-Woof.

It had been bad enough to be spanked for his disobedience, but Boxer had felt that he deserved this. He had bawled lustily and then he had whimpered softly all the way back to that tree in which Woof-Woof had obediently remained. Until he reached the foot of that tree and looked up at Woof-Woof, there had been no sulkiness in Boxer.

But when he saw Woof-Woof grinning down at him as if she were glad of all his trouble, Boxer suddenly felt that he was the most abused little Bear in all the Great World.

"Don't you wish you hadn't tried to be so smart?" whispered Woof-Woof, when at Mother Bear's command she had joined Boxer on the ground. "I heard you bawling. I guess next time you'll be good like me."

This was too much for Boxer, and he struck at Woof-Woof.

Instantly he felt the sting of Mother Bear's big paw. It made him squeal. Woof-Woof grinned at him again, but she took care that Mother Bear shouldn't see that grin.

Woof-Woof actually seemed to enjoy seeing Boxer in trouble. Little folks and some big ones often are that way.

So, because with Mother Bear there he had no chance to show his spite to Woof-Woof, Boxer sulked. He wanted to be by himself just to pity himself. Instead of walking close at the heels of Mother Bear as usual, he allowed Woof-Woof to take that place, and he tagged on behind just as far back as he dared to. Once in a while Woof-Woof would turn her head and make a face at him. Boxer pretended not to see this.

When they stopped to rest, Boxer curled up by himself and pretended to have a nap, while all the time he was just sulking. When after a while Woof-Woof tried to make friends with him, he would have nothing to do with her. Boxer was actually having a good time being miserable. People can get that way sometimes.

Finally Mother Bear lost patience and sent him in under the great windfall to the bedroom where he was born. "Stay in there until you get over being sulky," said she. "Don't put foot outside until you can be pleasant."

So Boxer crept under the great windfall to the bedroom where he had spent his babyhood. There he curled up and was more sulky then ever. He said to himself that he hated Mother Bear and he hated his sister, Woof-Woof. He didn't do anything of the kind. He loved both dearly. But he tried to make himself believe that he hated them. People in the sulks are very fond of doing things like that.

So while Woof-Woof went over to the Laughing Brook with Mother Bear, under the great windfall Boxer lay and sulked and tried to think of some way of getting even with Mother Bear and Woof-Woof.

XXIV. Boxer Starts Out To Get Even

Wait a minute; count the cost.
Wasted time is time that's lost.
Mother Bear.

BOXER lay curled up in a corner of the bedroom under the great windfall, and there he sulked and sulked and sulked and tried to make himself believe he was the worst treated little Bear in all the Great World. But sulking all alone isn't any fun at all. No one can truly enjoy being sulky, with no one to see it. So in spite of himself Boxer was soon wondering what Woof-Woof and Mother Bear were doing. He had seen them start off toward the Laughing Brook and though he wouldn't own up to it, even to himself, he wished that he was with them. He dearly loved to play along the Laughing Brook.

When he could stand it no longer, Boxer stole out to the entrance and poked his head out from under the great windfall. There he stood for the longest time looking, listening, smelling. Everything looked just as usual. There were no strange sounds. The Merry Little Breezes brought him no new smells. There were no signs of Mother Bear and Woof-Woof. He didn't know whether they had gone up the Laughing Brook or down the Laughing Brook. He tried to pretend that he didn't care where they were or what they were doing.

But he didn't succeed. You know it isn't often you can really and truly fool yourself. You may fool other people, but not yourself. So after a while Boxer gave up trying to pretend he didn't care. And then sulkiness gave way to temper, bad temper.

56

"I-I-I'll go way, way off in the Great World and never come back. Then I guess Mother Bear and Woof-Woof will be sorry and wish they had been good to me," muttered Boxer.

He stood up for an instant to look and listen. Then that silly little Bear scampered off as fast as he could go, without paying any attention at all to his direction. His one thought was to get as far as possible from the great windfall before Mother Bear should return. He would show Mother Bear that he was too big to be spanked and sent to bed. He would show Woof-Woof that he could take care of himself and didn't need to tag along after Mother Bear.

So Boxer ran and ran until his little legs grew tired. The only use he made of his eyes was to keep looking behind him to see if Mother Bear was after him. Not once did he use them to take note of the way in which he was going. So it was that when at last he stopped, because his legs ached and he was out of breath, Boxer was as completely lost as a little Bear could be. He didn't know it then, but he was. He was to find it out later.

"Now," said Boxer, talking to himself as he rested, "I guess Mother Bear will be sorry she spanked me. And I guess Woof-Woof will wish she hadn't laughed at me and made fun of me. Maybe they'll be so sorry they'll cry. If they come to look for me, I'll hide where they won't ever find me. Then they'll be sorrier than ever and I'll be even with them. I won't go home until I am as big as my father, Buster Bear. Then I guess they'll treat me nice."

So Boxer rested and planned the wonderful things he would do out in the Great World and was glad he had run away from home. You see, it was very pleasant there in the Green Forest, and after all, if he really wanted to, he could go back home. That is what he thought, anyway. You see, he hadn't the least idea yet that he was lost.

XXV. Chatterer Has Fun with Boxer

Who does not fear to take a chance
Will make the most of circumstance.
Mother Bear.

THAT is Chatterer all over. In all the Green Forest there
is no one who appears to enjoy mischief so thoroughly
as does Chatterer the Red Squirrel. And there is no one
more ready to take a chance when it offers.

It happened that Chatterer discovered Boxer, the runaway little Bear, as he rested and planned what he would
do out in the Great World. Chatterer kept quiet until he
was sure that Boxer was alone; that Mother Bear and
Woof-Woof were nowhere near. When he was sure of this,
Chatterer guessed just what had happened. He guessed
that Boxer had run away. You know Chatterer is one of the
sharpest and shrewdest of all the little people in the
Green Forest.

Chatterer grinned. "I believe," said he to himself, "that
that silly little Bear has run away and is lost. If he isn't
lost, he ought to be, and I'll see to it that he is. Yes, Sir, I'll
see to it that he is properly lost. This is my chance to get
even for the fright he and his sister gave me when they
chased me up a tree."

Chatterer once more looked everywhere to make sure
no one else was about. Then he lightly jumped over into
the tree under which Boxer was sitting. He took care to
make no sound. He crept out on a limb directly over Boxer
and then he dropped a pine cone.

The pine cone hit Boxer right on the end of his nose,
and because his nose is rather tender, it hurt. It made the

58

tears come. Then, too, it was so unexpected it startled Boxer. "Ouch!" he cried, as he sprang to one side and looked up to see where that cone had come from.

When he saw Chatterer grinning down at him, Boxer grew very angry. That was the same fellow he once had so nearly caught in a tree top. This time he would catch him. Down came another cone on Boxer's head.

"Can't catch me! Can't catch me!" taunted Chatterer, in the most provoking way.

Boxer growled and started up that tree. "Can't catch a flea! Can't catch me!" cried Chatterer gleefully, as he looked down at Boxer and made faces at him.

He waited until Boxer was halfway up that tree then lightly ran out to the end of a branch and leaped across to a branch of the next tree. From there he called Boxer all sorts of names and made fun of him until the little Bear was so angry he hardly knew what he was doing. Of course he couldn't jump across as Chatterer had. He was too big to run out on a branch that way, even had he dared try it. So there was nothing to do but to scramble down that tree and climb the next one.

Boxer started down. When he reached the ground, he found Chatterer also on the ground. "Can't catch a flea! Can't catch me!" shouted Chatterer more provokingly than ever.

"I can catch any Red Squirrel that lives," growled Boxer and jumped at Chatterer. Chatterer dodged and ran, Boxer after him. Around trees and stumps, this way, that way and the other way, over logs, behind piles of brush Chatterer led Boxer, until the latter was so out of breath he had to stop.

Chatterer chuckled. "I guess that now he is quite properly lost," said he to himself, as he ran up a tree and dropped another cone on Boxer. "I guess I've turned him around so many times he hasn't any idea where home is or anything else, for that matter. I haven't had so much fun for a long time."

He dropped another cone on Boxer and then started off through the tree tops, leaving Boxer all alone.

XXVI. Alone and Lost in the Great World

> He truly brave is who can be
> No whit less brave with none to see.
> *Mother Bear.*

SOMEHOW it is easier to be brave when there are others about to see how brave you are. It is a great deal easier. To be brave when you are all alone is quite another matter. That is real bravery. And to be alone and lost and brave is the greatest bravery.

When Chatterer the Red Squirrel raced away through the tree tops, leaving Boxer alone to recover his breath and rest his weary little legs, he left a little Bear as completely lost as ever a little Bear had been since the beginning of the Great World. Boxer didn't know it then. He was too busy getting his breath and thinking how good it was to rest to think of anything else.

But after awhile Boxer felt quite himself again, and once more his anger at Chatterer the Red Squirrel began to rise. Boxer looked all about for Chatterer. There was no sign of him. Boxer swelled up with a feeling of importance.

"That fellow must be hiding. I guess I've given him a scare he won't forget in a hurry," boasted Boxer. How that would have tickled Chatterer had he heard it.

Now that Chatterer had disappeared, Boxer began to wonder what he should do next. It suddenly came to him that he was in a strange place. None of the trees or stumps about there was familiar. There wasn't a single familiar thing to be seen anywhere. A queer feeling of uneasiness crept over Boxer. He couldn't sit still. No, sir, he couldn't sit still. He didn't know why, but he couldn't.

So Boxer started on aimlessly. He had nothing in particular to do and nowhere in particular to go.

Presently he noticed the first of the Black Shadows creeping through the Green Forest. Somehow those Black Shadows made him think of home. Probably Mother Bear and Woof-Woof were back there by this time. He wondered if they had missed him and would start looking for him. If he didn't see them, how would he ever know whether or not they looked for him? How would he ever know if he really did get even with them by making them anxious? Why not go back near the great windfall and watch?

"Of course I won't go home," muttered Boxer to himself, as he shuffled along. "I've left home for good. I'll just go back and hide near there where I can watch and see all that happens. It will be great fun to watch Mother Bear and Woof-Woof hunt for me. I guess I'll hurry a little," he added, as he noticed how the creeping Black Shadows had increased. So Boxer began to run.

"I didn't think home was so far," he panted at last, looking fearfully over his shoulder at the Black Shadows. "Ha, there is the great windfall!" he added joyously, as he spied a pile of fallen trees in the distance.

He approached it carefully, stopping often to look and listen, for you know he didn't want to be seen by Mother Bear or Woof-Woof. At least, he thought he didn't want to be seen by them, though way down inside that was just what he did want.

He heard no one and saw no one. Presently he was close to that windfall. A great longing for home swept over him. He no longer wanted to get even with anybody. All he wanted was home and mother. Perhaps Mother Bear and Woof-Woof hadn't returned yet and he could slip in. Then they would never know. Boxer slipped around the old windfall to where he thought the entrance was. There wasn't any! It wasn't the right windfall! Boxer knew right then and there that he was lost, that he was a lone, lost little Bear out in the Great World. He sat down and began to cry.

XXVII. A Dreadful Night for a Little Bear

A lot of people, great and small,
  Are like a frightened little Bear—
Where danger there is none at all
  They somehow get a dreadful scare.
                    Mother Bear.

MORE and more Black Shadows crept through the Green Forest and all around Boxer, the lone, lost little Bear, as he sat crying and wishing with all his might that he never, never had thought of running away. He wanted to be back in the great windfall which had been his home. He wanted Mother Bear. "Boo, hoo, hoo," sobbed the little Bear, "I would just as soon have a spanking. I wouldn't mind it at all if only I had my Mother. Boo, hoo, hoo."

Now there are many keen ears in the Green Forest after dark, and no one can cry there and not be heard. Hooty the Owl was the first to hear those sobs, and on wings that made no sound at all he flew to see what was the matter. Perched on top of a tall stump just back of Boxer, it didn't take Hooty long to understand that this little Bear was lost.

"He needs a lesson," thought Hooty. "He needs a lesson. He must have run away from home. There is nothing around here for him to fear, but it will be a good thing for him to think there is. Here goes to give him a scare he won't forget in a hurry."

Hooty drew a long breath and then hooted as only he can. It was so sudden, so loud and so fierce, that it was enough to frighten even one accustomed to it. Boxer, who never had heard that call close at hand before, was so frightened he lost his balance and fell over on his back, his legs waving helplessly. But he didn't stay on his back. I should say not! In a twinkling he was on his feet and running pell-mell.

Again rang out Hooty's terrible hunting call, and Boxer was sure that it was right at his heels. As a matter of fact, Hooty had not moved from the tall stump. Headlong Boxer raced through the woods. And because it was quite dark and because he was trying to look behind him, instead of watching where he was going, he pitched heels over head down the bank of the Laughing Brook, splash into a little pool where Billy Mink was fishing. The tumble and the wetting frightened the little Bear more than ever, and Billy Mink's angry snarl didn't make him feel any better. Without so much as a glance at Billy Mink, he scrambled to his feet and up the bank, sure that a new and terrible enemy was at his heels.

More heedlessly than ever he raced through the Green Forest and just by chance entered the thicket where Mrs. Lightfoot the Deer had a certain wonderful secret. Mrs. Lightfoot jumped, making a crash of brush.

"Oh-oo," moaned Boxer, dodging to one side and continuing headlong. When he could run no more, he crept under a pile of brush and there he spent the rest of the night, the most dreadful night he ever had known or was likely ever to know again. Old Man Coyote happened along and yelled as only he can, and unless you know what it is, that sound is quite dreadful. Boxer never had heard it close at hand before, and he didn't recognize it. He was sure that only a great and terrible creature could make such a dreadful noise, and he shook with fear for an hour after.

So all night long the little Bear heard strange sounds and imagined dreadful things and couldn't get a wink of sleep. And all the time not once was any real danger near him. There wasn't a single thing to be afraid of.

He pitched heels over head down the bank of the Laughing Brook.

XXVIII. Boxer Gets His Own Breakfast

> True independence he has earned
> Who for himself to do has learned.
> *Mother Bear.*

IT seemed to Boxer, the lost little Bear, that that dreadful night would last forever; that it never would end. Of course, it didn't last any longer than a night at that season of the year usually does, and it wasn't dreadful at all. The truth is, it was an unusually fine night, and everybody but Boxer and anxious Mother Bear thought so.

Perhaps you can guess just how glad Boxer was to see the Jolly Little Sunbeams chase the Black Shadows out of the Green Forest the next morning. He still felt frightened and very, very lonesome, but things looked very different by daylight, and he felt very much braver and bolder.

First of all, he took a nap. All night he had been awake, for he had been too frightened to sleep. That nap did him a world of good. When he awoke, he felt quite like another Bear. And the first thing he thought of was breakfast.

Now always before Mother Bear had furnished Boxer with his breakfast and with all his other meals. But there was no Mother Bear to do it this morning, and his stomach was very empty. If anything were to be put in it, he was the one who would have to put it there.

Just thinking of breakfast made Boxer hungrier than ever. He couldn't lie still. He must have something to eat, and he must have it soon. He crawled out from under the pile of brush, shook himself, and tried to decide where to go in search of a breakfast. But being lost, of course he had no idea which way to turn.

"I guess it doesn't make much difference," grumbled Boxer. "Whichever way I go, I guess I'll find something to eat if I keep going long enough."

So Boxer started out. And because he had something on his mind, something to do, he forgot that he was lonesome, and he forgot to be afraid. He just couldn't think of anything but breakfast. Now while he never had had to get food for himself before, Boxer had watched Mother Bear getting food and felt that he knew just how to go about it.

He found a thoroughly rotted old stump and pulled it apart. It happened that he found nothing there to eat. But a few minutes later he forgot all about this disappointment as he pulled over a small log and saw ants scurrying in every direction. He promptly swept them into his mouth with his tongue and smacked his lips at the taste of them. He didn't leave that place until not another ant was to be seen.

By and by he dug out certain tender little roots and ate them. How he knew where to dig for them, he couldn't have told himself. He just knew, that was all. Something inside him prompted him to stop and dig, and he did so.

Once he chased a Wood Mouse into a hole and wasted a lot of time trying to dig him out. But it was exciting and a lot of fun, so he didn't mind much, even when he had to give up. He caught three or four beetles and near the Laughing Brook surprised a young frog. Altogether he made a very good breakfast. And because he got it all himself, with no help from any one, he enjoyed it more than any breakfast he could remember. And suddenly he felt quite a person of the Great World and quite equal to taking care of himself. He forgot that he had cried for his mother only the night before. The Great World wasn't such a bad place after all.

XXIX. Boxer Has a Painful Lesson

Don't judge a stranger by his looks,
  Lest they may prove to be deceiving.
The stupid-looking may be smart
  In ways you'll find beyond believing.
                                  Mother Bear.

HAVING succeeded in getting his own breakfast, and a very good one at that, Boxer felt quite set up, as the saying is. He felt chesty. That is to say, he felt big, self-important, independent. For a little cub who had cried most of the night from loneliness and fear, Boxer showed a surprising change. The light of day, a full stomach, and the feeling that he was able to take care of himself had made a new Bear of that little cub. Anyway he felt so and thought so.

"I'm not afraid of anybody or anything," boasted the foolish little Bear to himself, as he wandered along through the Green Forest. "I'm glad I left home. I'm glad I am out in the Great World. I guess I know about all there is to know. Anyway, I guess I know all there is any need of knowing."

As he said this, Boxer stood up and swelled himself out and looked so funny that Prickly Porky the Porcupine, who happened along just then, just had to chuckle down inside, and this is something that Prickly Porky seldom does.

"That little rascal must have run away from his mother, and he thinks he is smart and knows all there is to know. I don't believe that even Mother Bear could tell him anything just now. She would be wasting her breath. He needs

67

a lesson or two in practical experience. I believe I'll give him one just for his own good," thought Prickly Porky.

There was something almost like a twinkle in Prickly Porky's usually dull eyes as he slowly waddled straight toward Boxer. Boxer heard the rustle of Prickly Porky's tail dragging through the leaves and turned to see who was coming. What he saw was, of course, the stupidest-looking fellow in all the Green Forest.

It was the first time Boxer had seen Prickly Porky, and he had no idea who he was. Boxer stood up and stared in the rudest and most impolite manner. He wasn't afraid. This fellow was no bigger than he, and he was too stupid-looking and too slow to be dangerous.

Boxer was standing in a narrow little path, and Prickly Porky was coming up this little path straight toward him. One of them would have to step aside for the other. It didn't enter Boxer's head that he should be that one. As Prickly Porky drew near, Boxer growled a warning. It was the best imitation of Mother Bear's deep, grumbly-rumbly growl that Boxer could manage. It was hard work for Prickly Porky to keep from laughing right out when he heard it.

But he acted just as if he didn't hear it. He kept right on. Then he pretended to see Boxer for the first time. "Step aside, little cub, step aside and let me pass," said he.

To be called "little cub" just when he was feeling so important and grown-up was more than Boxer could stand. His little eyes grew red with anger.

"Step aside yourself," he growled. "Step aside yourself, if you don't want to get hurt."

Prickly Porky didn't step aside. He kept right on coming. He didn't hurry, and he didn't appear to be in the least afraid. It was plain that he expected Boxer to get out of his way. Boxer drew back his lips and showed all his little white teeth. Then he slowly reached out one paw and prepared to strike Prickly Porky on the side of the head if he came any nearer.

XXX. Boxer Is Sadder but Much Wiser

Experience is not a preacher,
But has no equal as a teacher.
Mother Bear.

SAMMY Jay happened along in the Green Forest just in time to see the meeting between Boxer and Prickly Porky the Porcupine. He saw at once that this was the first time Boxer had seen Prickly Porky, and that he had no idea who this fellow in the path was.

"If that little Bear has any sense at all, he'll be polite and get out of Prickly Porky's way," muttered Sammy. "But I'm afraid he hasn't any sense. He looks to me all puffed up, as if he thinks he knows all there is to know. He'll find out he doesn't in just about a minute if he stays there. Hi, there! Don't do that! Don't hit him!"

This last was screamed at Boxer, who had stretched out a paw as if to strike Prickly Porky as soon as he was near enough. But the warning came too late. Prickly Porky had kept right on coming along that little path, and just as Sammy Jay screamed, Boxer struck.

"Wow!" yelled Boxer, dancing about and holding up one paw, the paw with which he had struck at Prickly Porky, and on his face was such a look of amazement that Sammy Jay laughed so that he nearly tumbled from his perch.

"Wow, Wow!" yelled Boxer, still dancing about and shaking that paw.

"Pull it out. Pull it out at once, before it gets in deeper," commanded Sammy Jay, when he could stop laughing long enough.

"Pull what out?" asked Boxer rather sullenly, for he didn't like being laughed at. No one does when in trouble.

"That little spear that is sticking in your paw," replied Sammy. "If you don't, you'll have a terribly sore paw."

Boxer looked at his paw. Sure enough, there was one of Prickly Porky's little spears. He took hold of it with his teeth and started to pull. Then he let go and shook his paw. "Wow! that hurts!" he cried, the tears in his eyes.

"Of course it hurts," replied Sammy Jay. "And if you don't do as I tell you and pull it out now, it will hurt a great deal more. That paw will get so sore you can't use it. It is a lucky thing for you, young fellow, that you were in too much of a hurry and struck too soon. If you had waited a second longer, you would have filled your paw with those little spears. What were you thinking of, anyway? Don't you know that no one ever interferes with Prickly Porky? It never pays to. Even Buster Bear, big as he is, is polite to Prickly Porky."

Boxer sat down and looked at his paw carefully. That little spear, or quill, was right in the tenderest part. It must be pulled out. Sammy Jay was right about that. Boxer shut his teeth on that little spear and jerked back his head quick and hard. Out came the little spear. Boxer whimpered a little as he licked the place where the little spear had been. After he had licked it a minute or two, that paw felt better.

Meanwhile Prickly Porky had paid no attention whatever to the little Bear. He had slowly waddled on up the little path, quite as if no one were about. He was attending strictly to his own business. But inside he was chuckling.

"That scamp got off easy," he muttered. "It would have been a good thing for him if he had had a few more of those little spears to pull out. I guess that in the future he will take care to leave me alone. There is nothing like teaching the young to respect their elders."

XXXI. Boxer Meets a Polite Little Fellow

Because another is polite
Pray do not think he cannot fight.
Mother Bear.

THE memories of little folks are short, so far as their troubles are concerned. Hardly was Boxer, the runaway little Bear, out of sight of Prickly Porky the Porcupine than his eyes, ears and nose were so busy trying to discover new things that he hardly thought of his recent trouble. To be sure that paw from which he had pulled one of Prickly Porky's little spears was sore, but not enough so to worry him much. And there were so many other things to think about that he couldn't waste time on troubles that were over.

So the little Bear wandered this way and that way, as something new caught his eyes or some strange sound demanded to be looked into. He was having a wonderful time, for he felt that he was indeed out in the Great World and it was a wonderful and beautiful place. If he thought of his twin sister, Woof-Woof, at all, it was to pity her tagging along at Mother Bear's heels and doing only those things which Mother Bear said she could.

By and by something white moving about near an old stump caught his attention. At once he hurried over to satisfy his curiosity. When he got near enough he discovered a little fellow dressed in black-and-white. He had a big plumy tail and he was very busy minding his own business. He hardly glanced at Boxer.

Boxer stared at him for a few minutes. "Hello," he ventured finally.

71

"Good morning. It is a fine morning, isn't it?" said the little stranger politely.

"What are you doing?" demanded the little Bear rudely.

"Just minding my own business," replied the little stranger pleasantly. "Where is your mother?"

"I don't know and I don't care. I've left home," said Boxer, trying to look big and important.

"You don't say!" exclaimed the little stranger. "Aren't you rather small to be starting out alone in the Great World?"

Now Boxer was so much bigger than this little stranger in black-and-white, and the little stranger was so very polite, that already Boxer felt that the little stranger must be afraid of him. All Boxer's previous feeling of bigness and importance came back to him. He wanted to show off. He wanted this little stranger to respect him. To have that stranger suggest that he was rather small to be out alone in the Great World hurt Boxer's pride. In fact, it made him angry.

"If I were as small as you, perhaps I would feel that way," retorted Boxer rudely.

"I didn't use the right word. I should have said young instead of small," explained the stranger mildly. "Of course, I am small compared with you, but I am fully grown and have been out in the Great World a long time, while you are very young and just starting out. I wonder if your mother knows where you are."

"It is none of your business whether my mother knows or not," retorted Boxer more rudely than before, for he was growing more and more angry.

"Certainly not. I haven't said it was," replied the stranger, still speaking politely. "I am not in the least interested. Besides, I know anyway. I know that she doesn't know. I know that you have run away, and I know that you have some bitter lessons to learn before you will be fitted to live by yourself in the Great World. If you will just step aside, I will be much obliged. There is a big piece of bark just back of you under which there may be some fat beetles."

XXXII. Boxer Wishes He Hadn't

This is, you'll find, the law of fate:
Regrets are always just too late.
Mother Bear.

SAMMY Jay had followed Boxer, for he felt sure that things were bound to happen wherever that little Bear was. So Sammy saw his meeting with Jimmy Skunk. He saw how polite Jimmy was and how very impolite the little Bear was.

Sammy understood perfectly. He knew that probably Boxer knew nothing at all about Jimmy Skunk and never had heard of that little bag of scent carried by Jimmy and dreaded by all of Jimmy's neighbors. He knew that the little Bear was rude, simply because he was so much bigger than Jimmy Skunk that he could see no reason for being polite, especially as Jimmy had asked him to do something he didn't want to do.

When Jimmy Skunk began to lose patience, Sammy Jay thought it was time for him to give Boxer a little advice. "Don't be silly! Do as Jimmy Skunk tells you to, or you will be the sorriest little Bear that ever lived!" screamed Sammy, as he saw Jimmy's great plume of a tail begin to go up, which is Jimmy's signal of danger.

But Boxer, foolish little Bear that he was, couldn't see anything to fear from one so much smaller than he. So he paid no attention to Jimmy's request that he step aside. Instead he laughed in the most impudent way.

"Run! Run!" screamed Sammy Jay.

Boxer didn't move. Jimmy Skunk stamped angrily with his front feet. Then something happened. Yes, sir, something happened. It was so sudden and so unexpected that Boxer didn't know exactly what had happened, but he was very much aware that it *had* happened. Something was in his eyes and made them smart and for a few minutes blinded him. Something was choking him; it seemed to him he could hardly breathe. And there was the most awful odor he ever had smelled.

Boxer rolled over and over and over on the ground. He was trying to get away from that awful odor. But he couldn't. He couldn't, for the very good reason that he carried it along with him. You see, Jimmy Skunk had punished that silly little Bear by throwing on him a little of that powerful scent he always carries with him to use in time of danger or when provoked.

"What did I tell you? What did I tell you?" screamed Sammy Jay. "I guess you won't interfere with Jimmy Skunk again in a hurry. It serves you right. It serves you just right. But it is hard on the people who live about here. Yes, sir, it is hard on them to have all the sweetness of the Green Forest spoiled by that scent of Jimmy Skunk's. I can't stand it myself, so I'll be moving along. It serves you right, you silly little Bear. It serves you right." With this Sammy Jay flew away.

Boxer knew then that Jimmy Skunk had been the cause of this new and dreadful trouble he was in, and great respect mingled with fear took possession of him. And oh, how Boxer wished that he hadn't been impolite! How he wished he hadn't refused to do as Jimmy Skunk had politely asked him to!

"I wish I hadn't! I wish I hadn't! I wish I hadn't!" sobbed Boxer over and over, as he tried to get away from that dreadful smell and couldn't.

XXXIII. Woof-Woof Turns Up Her Nose

I pray you be not one of those
Who boast the scornful turned-up nose.
Mother Bear.

NOW all the time that Boxer had been losing himself more and more and getting into more and more trouble, Mother Bear had been worrying about him, and she and his twin sister, Woof-Woof, had been everywhere but the right place looking for him.

You remember that Mother Bear and Woof-Woof had been away from home when Boxer decided to run away. When they returned, Boxer had been gone so long that Mother Bear's nose failed to find enough of his scent to follow. So when she started to look for him, she started in the wrong direction. Of course, she had to take Woof-Woof with her, and because Woof-Woof got tired after a while, Mother Bear couldn't hunt as thoroughly as she would have done had she been alone.

At first Woof-Woof felt very badly indeed at the loss of her little twin brother. Down in her heart she admired him for his boldness in running away, but when she thought of all the dreadful things that might happen to him out in the Great World, she became very sorrowful. This was at first. After she had tramped and tramped and tramped behind Mother Bear, tramped until her feet ached, she became cross. She blamed Boxer, and quite rightly, for those aching feet. The more they ached the crosser she became, until she tried to make herself believe that she didn't care what happened to that heedless brother.

"I don't care if I never see him again," she grumbled. "I

75

don't care what happens to him. Whatever happens will serve him right. I wish Mother Bear would remember that my legs are not as long as hers. I'm tired. I want to rest. I want to rest, I do. I want to rest. Ouch! My feet are getting sore."

Now such news as Jimmy Skunk's punishment of Boxer travels fast through the Green Forest, and it wasn't long before the story of it reached Mrs. Bear's ears. She growled dreadful threats of what she would do if she met Jimmy Skunk, though she knew very well that she would politely step aside if she did meet him, and then she started for the place where Boxer had been given his lessons in politeness by Jimmy Skunk.

There was no doubt about the place when they reached it. "Phew!" cried Woof-Woof, holding her nose.

Mother Bear merely grunted and started off faster than before. Woof-Woof had to run to keep up with her. Mother Bear had that smell to guide her now. She knew that all she had to do now to find her runaway son was to follow up that smell.

So it was that just as the Black Shadows were beginning to creep through the Green Forest, and poor little Boxer, a very lonely, miserable and frightened little Bear, was beginning to dread another night, he heard a crashing in the brush, and out came Mother Bear and Woof-Woof. With a glad squeal of joy, Boxer started to run toward them. But a growl, such an ugly growl, from Mother Bear stopped him.

"Don't you come near us," said she. "You can follow us, but don't you dare come a step nearer than you are now. It would serve you right if we had nothing more to do with you, but after all, you are rather small to be wandering about alone. Besides, there is no knowing what more disgrace you would get us into. Now come along."

Boxer looked at Woof-Woof for some sign of sympathy. But Woof-Woof held her head very high and turned up her nose at him. "Phew!" said she.

XXXIV. All Is Well at Last

If you are taught not to forget
Your punishment you'll ne'er regret.
            Mother Bear.

MRS. Bear is one of those mothers who believe in punishment. She believes that the cub who is never punished for wrong-doing is almost sure to grow up to be of little or no use in the Great World, provided he lives to grow up at all. She doubts if he will live to grow up at all. So her cubs are promptly punished when they disobey or do wrong, and they are punished in a way to make them remember.

Now when Boxer, the lost little cub who had had such a dreadful time, saw Mother Bear and his sister Woof-Woof, he thought all his troubles were at an end. Perhaps you can guess what his feelings were when he was stopped short by a growl from Mother Bear. He wanted—oh, how he wanted—to rush up to her and snuggle against her and feel her big paws gently patting him.

But there was to be none of that. It was plain that Mother Bear meant exactly what she said when she told him to come no nearer. And when he looked at his twin sister, Woof-Woof, she turned up her nose and it was quite clear that she wanted nothing to do with him.

Poor little Boxer. He didn't understand it at all at first. You see, in the joy of being found, he had forgotten that he still carried that dreadful scent with which Jimmy Skunk had punished him, and so no one, not even his mother or sister, would want him very near. When Woof-Woof cried "Phew!" as she turned up her nose he remem-

77

bered. He hung his head and meekly shuffled along after his mother and sister, taking care to get no nearer to them. He didn't dare to, for every few steps Mother Bear would swing her head around and grumble a warning.

And this was just the beginning of Boxer's punishment. Day after day he tagged along, far behind, but always keeping his mother and sister in sight. You may be sure he took care to do that. He had had quite enough of seeing the Great World alone. Not for anything would he be lost again. But it was hard, very hard, to have only what was left when Mother Bear found a feast. What he didn't know was that Mother Bear always took care that there should be a fair share left. At such times Woof-Woof took great joy in smacking her lips while Boxer sat up watching from a distance.

When they slept Boxer had to curl up by himself. At first this was the hardest of all. But little by little he got used to it. He didn't know and Woof-Woof didn't know, but Mother Bear did, that this was good for him; it was making him more and more sure of himself. And tagging along behind as he did every day was doing the same thing. He was always looking for something that Mother Bear and Woof-Woof might have missed. And so he learned to use his eyes and his nose and his ears better than Woof-Woof did, for she depended more on Mother Bear, being right at her heels.

As the days passed, Boxer's coat became more and more free from that dreadful scent. Boxer had become so used to it that he didn't notice it at all, so he wasn't conscious when it began to grow less. At last it got so that it was hardly to be noticed except on rainy or very damp days. For a long time after Mother Bear had permitted him to resume his place with Woof-Woof, she drove him away on such days.

So at last Boxer's punishment ended. Mother Bear gave him a good talking to and said that she hoped this would be a lesson he never would forget. "Yes'm, it will," he had replied very meekly, and he knew it would. Then he took his place once more, save that now, instead of following at Mother Bear's heels, he allowed Woof-Woof to do that and he followed her. Though Woof-Woof didn't suspect it, he preferred it so.

So Buster Bear's twins grew and grew until every one said that they were the finest young Bears ever seen in the Green Forest.

Billy Mink says that these cubs have received attention enough and that there are other people who should be considered. Perhaps Billy is right, though I suspect he is thinking of himself. Anyway this ends the Green Forest series and the next book will be the first in the Smiling Pool series. The title will be Billy Mink.*

*NOTE: *The Adventures of Billy Mink* is not published by Dover Publications.